Anomaly Jane

by

Lincoln Keene

Cover by GoOnWrite.com

ANOMALY JANE

BY LINCOLN KEENE

Copyright 2021 Lincoln Keene

TABLE OF CONTENTS

CHAPTER ONE

LYDE ISRAEL HAD been a soldier, and a good one. He had been a member of the famous all-black cavalry unit, the Buffalo Soldiers, chasing the Indians around the prairie after the War.

After that, Clyde had been a husband and a father, and he thought he had done a pretty good job at that too. Leastways until the cholera swept the plains that terrible winter and took his wife and baby son. After that there was nothing left important enough to be good at.

So Clyde Israel had become a drunk. Anybody can be good at that. All you need is practice.

He must 'a got plenty of practice last night, he reflected sourly.

Judging by how much he didn't remember, not even falling asleep here in the alley between the saloon and the stage station. Or passing out, whichever. Didn't much matter.

Another clue to how much drinking he must've done the night before could be found in the horrible taste invading his mouth. Something like as if a sick, diseased rat had crawled in there and died. Several weeks ago.

Oh, well, every day was a new beginning, Clyde told

himself. This was his third or fourth day in this small Arizona town, and so far he liked it. Might stay as much a week, even two if he could find some day work. Clyde paid a visit to the outhouse behind the saloon, then ambled up front to the watering trough, empty this early in the morning. He pumped himself a nice full bucket of clean water, still cool. The outside temperature wouldn't pass ninety degrees for several hours yet.

Clyde drank his fill, using the ladle which was always kept hanging from a nail near the pump just for that purpose. Then he poured the rest of the bucket over his head and chest, wiping himself down as best he could with his ratty old bandanna. His shirt would dry in no time as the day heated up.

Ablutions completed, Clyde, looking around to make sure the street was still empty, cautiously took a seat on one of the two wooden rocking chairs on the porch in front of the saloon. Even ten years and more after the nation fought a war to make sure ALL men were free, a black man still had to be careful where he sat. Sit in a white man's chair or walk into a white-only saloon and you might get a beating from him and his friends. And that type always traveled in packs.

Since the saloon didn't open until noontime, Clyde felt pretty safe. He leaned back in the comfortable rocker and closed his eyes, not really sleeping but not quite awake either.

Around him the dusty little town started to wake up. Up the street somewhere a chicken proudly announced her production of an egg. Someone led a horse slowly clopping to the trough and pumped it's morning drink, then led it back up the street. Two doors down the man who ran the General Store was sweeping his front walk.

Next door to the saloon, the door to the stage station opened and Mister Newton, the agent, came out. He was carrying a steaming cup of coffee in each hand. He strolled over to Clyde.

"Good morning to you, Mister Israel!" he said cheerfully. "I saw you out here enjoyin' the mornin' and thought perhaps you wouldn't mind me joinin' you for coffee.

Stage isn't due for an hour. That's if it's on time." He held out a fragrant mug, which Clyde accepted reverently. He was oddly moved by the simple gesture of friendship.

Newton was one of those rare men who only saw others as men, not as white men or black men.

The two men sat in their chairs in companionable enough silence for a while, sipping happily.

"Nice little town you got here," ventured Clyde finally. "Friendly."

Newton nodded thoughtfully. "Every town has its' good ones and its' bad ones," he pontificated finally, "but it does seem like we lucked out and got more than our share of good ones. The marshall, the doc, the blacksmith...bunch more I could name, all good, solid, hard working people."

Newton was himself one of the good ones. Besides bringing Clyde the coffee—which was terrific!—he also offered to pay Clyde for a few hours' labor after the stagecoach left. The eight-horse team the stage would be leaving behind would need to be rubbed down, inspected thoroughly for cuts, bruises, swelling, stones in hooves, and the like, and then watered and grained. And then stabled. His stagehand had the day off, he said, and he'd be obliged for the help.

CHAPTER TWO

AN HOUR LATER, not very much had changed. There were four or five people at the stage station, mostly milling around on the walk, either coming to take the stage or to meet somebody coming in. They included a young couple with a three or four year old toddler.

Clyde was still sitting peacefully in his rocker at the saloon next door, although Newton had collected his empty mugs and gone back to the stage station. The stage arrived in a cloud of dust and curses from the driver. Three passengers got out to "stretch their legs" as the euphemism went, while the horses were being unharnessed and replaced with the fresh team.

The first two passengers, portly men in cheap suits and derby hats, were probably drummers. Traveling salesmen. The third passenger was a young lady, blonde-haired and wearing a modest dress and high button shoes that showed she was a lady, her outfit clean and new and obviously bought for traveling. She also wore a straw cowboy hat with a ribbon on the brim which on most women would have looked ridiculous but on her somehow just managed to look adorable. She had a reticule, a small ladies' handbag with long straps which was fashionable at the time, slung from one shoulder.

Clyde couldn't see her face from where he was sitting but something about the way the young lady moved and carried herself led him to suspect there was one seriously beautiful woman hidden under that hat brim.

The young lady and one of the drummers went inside the stage station. The second drummer was having a hugging and backslapping reunion with the toddler couple.

Clyde heaved himself up out of the rocking chair to go help the stagecoach driver unharness the team and turn them into the corral across the street.

Suddenly the loud drumming of hooves came from up the street. There was a town ordinance against galloping on the main street but some cowhands—usually drunk, but sometimes just rowdy—thought it was funny to ignore.

A quick sweeping glance around showed two hard-ridden horses, still a ways up the street but coming fast. In the stage station doorway directly across from him, the young blonde lady with the cowboy hat, looking horrified.

Following her gaze, Clyde was horrified too, when he saw the toddler, who had somehow escaped the stage station porch, lying in the middle of the street! For some reason the child had run out into the middle of the street and then tripped and fallen down. She was now lying directly in the path of the oncoming horsemen, who no doubt couldn't see her in all the dust their horses were throwing. She was crying, terrified, but making no move to escape.

Even as he started running, Clyde Israel knew there was

no way in hell an old black ex-Buffalo Soldier ex-husband ex-father current drunk could move fast enough to save the little girl and get clear. Mentally, he gave a philosophic shrug. If he saved the child but died in the process, so be it.

Sometimes, though—not often, in fact extremely rarely, but sometimes—miracles happen.

Clyde, running as fast as he could, gasping like a steam engine, grabbed the little girl by the collar and waistband and tossed her clear, falling to his knees in the process.

But instead of squishing him flat, for some reason the lead horse took it into his head to rear up onto his back legs, neighing loudly and pirouetting in almost a compete circle before coming down again on all fours, almost unseating the rider, avoiding Clyde and blocking him from the second horse also.

Clyde saw that the little girl was safely in the arms of her hysterical mother as he stumbled two steps and collapsed onto his knees on the boardwalk. He felt as though his heart might explode and he could not catch a breath.

A rough hand grabbed his shoulder. "The hell you mean jumpin' in front of my hoss like that, boy?" demanded the burly cowhand who had almost just killed him and the child. "I coulda got hurt, damn you! My hoss mighta' bust a leg!"

Clyde was still on his knees. The rider kicked him in the chest, knocking him onto his back. Then, either not knowing or not caring that Clyde was unarmed, he started to draw his holstered Colt .45.

"Might I trouble you for just a moment of your time?" a southern-accented female voice inquired sweetly.

The rider turned his head to see who was talking. Clyde, on his back on the ground, could see it was Cowboy Hat Girl, although her hat was now hanging behind her on its string. He instantly learned two things:

First, as he had suspected, Cowboy Hat Girl was seriously beautiful, with about the bluest eyes he had ever seen, eyes right now full of mischief, and, Second, Cowboy Hat Girl had a big shiny silver pistol held rock-steady in her dainty little fist, and it was aimed directly at the rider's right eyeball...

"Now that I have your attention," continued the young lady sweetly, "perhaps you might hand me that gunbelt while we converse, just to ensure things stay civilized."

The unshaven, dirty-looking cowhand reluctantly unbuckled his holstered Colt .45, which the young lady took left-handed. By now Clyde was back on his feet and brushing himself off. With a grin, the young lady hung the gunbelt over Clyde's shoulder Mexican-guerilla style. "Would you mind holding onto that, sir?" she inquired. "It's much too heavy for me."

Sure it is, though Clyde. My whole arm'd be tremblin' holdin' that pistol steady for that long, but you're cool as a cucumber. "Clyde."

"I beg your pardon?"

"My name is Clyde. You go to callin' a black man "sir" around here people start talkin' bad about you."

The young lady regarded him levelly for a minute, then smiled. "Well, sir, I generally believe in keeping my Smith and Wesson ready to hand and saying whatever I like.

However, I have a feeling we're going to be friends. So I will call you Clyde and you may call me—"

"ANOMALY JANE!" called out a hearty male voice from up the boardwalk.

The young lady closed her eyes for a moment. When she opened them she looked at Clyde. "I loathe that nickname, Clyde," she said. "Please call me by my real name, Genevieve, or just Gen."

"That's a right pretty name, Miss Genevieve. Why's this deputy walkin' toward us call you,uh Anonymous? Or whatever?"

"Long story, Clyde," she responded as she turned to face the deputy, a strapping, mustachioed man in his mid-twenties. "Hello, Deputy Fallon,"she greeted him.

The young man frowned. "I have asked you repeatedly to call me Josh."

"I'm aware of that, Deputy Fallon," she put her pistol back in the reticule hanging from her shoulder, "are you here to arrest our Reckless Horseman?"

The deputy burst out laughing when he got a look at her prisoner. "Well, well, Anomaly Jane strikes again!" he chortled. "Do you realize who you have here? This here desperado is Billy Tyler, wanted for stagecoach robbery. Funny part is, the reward is seventy five dollars and he only got twenty six in the robbery!"

The deputy sobered quickly. "This does present me with a problem, though. I'm supposed to be on that outbound stage to testify in a court case. I need a jailer."

"Clyde can do it!" announced Genevieve.

"No offense, uh, Clyde, but I've seen you around town the last week or so and you're generally drunk, and—"

"Clyde won't drink while he's working as your jailer," Genevieve interrupted.

"I won't?" asked Clyde. "He won't?" asked the deputy.

"No, he won't," said Genevieve firmly. She faced Clyde and looked him right in the eyes. "I can see in your eyes you've had losses," she told him earnestly, "but today you saved a little girl's life, and you've made at least one friend and maybe more, and you've got a chance at a steady job! Those are some pretty good wins in anybody's book!"

Clyde held his hand out to the deputy. "You got my word I'll stay sober while I'm working for you," he promised.

The deputy shook without hesitation. "Good enough for me."

CHAPTER THREE

———

CLYDE WAS SO busy for the next two hours he never even had time to think about drinking. First, while Miss Genevieve held the stagecoach, he and Deputy Fallon ("If Jane will not call me Josh, perhaps you will") locked up the prisoner in the tiny office/jail. Then the deputy gave Clyde a badge and keys and walked him next door to the Shoo Fly restaurant to introduce him as the new jailer. The Shoo Fly would be feeding Clyde and his prisoner and billing it to the town.

Deputy Fallon and Miss Genevieve left on the outbound stage. Clyde spent the next hour or so with Mister Newton, taking care of the horses left behind by the stagecoach. One by one, they rubbed them down, inspected them for cuts, swelling, hoof-stones and the like, and then walked them into the barn and stabled them. After all the horses had been seen to, they gave them water and grain.

The man who owned the General Store was sitting on a hay bale outside the barn waiting for Clyde.

He handed Clyde a package. "No offense, mister, but you look a little ratty to be representin' our town,—" he smiled, "not to mention the hero who saved my daughter!

Please take this along with my thanks and that of my wife! Her and my daughter reckon you're about ten feet tall, and I can't say as they're wrong!"

Astounded, Clyde could do nothing but mumble his thanks and take the package. Back in the marshalls office, he opened the package and found a complete outfit from the skin out, drawers, socks, black work pants, a new dark blue shirt and yellow bandanna. The pants and shirt fit perfectly.

Also in the package was a sheathed fighting knife, double edged, razor sharp and with a point like a needle. It could be worn as a boot knife or slung behind the neck on a thong. With the holstered .45 and fully stocked gunbelt he still had from Billy Tyler, Clyde was armed better than he had been since he left the cavalry. He wasted no time in heating up some water in the woodstove so he could shave and take a bath. Shaved, bathed, dressed in new clothes, boots, gunbelt and knife sheath freshly cleaned and polished, badge gleaming on his shirt, Clyde felt terrific. He walked over to the Shoo-Fly to get lunch for his prisoner, but to be honest he mostly wanted to show off his new look.

When the waitress brought over Billy's lunch, all packed up, she pointed out a small package wrapped in brown butcher paper. "My boss lady put in a piece of fresh-made apple pie for you, Deputy," she told him. "On the house."

When Clyde looked toward the kitchen, he found quite an attractive middle-aged black lady smiling back at him. "Thanks, ma'am," he grinned as he left.

Walking back along the boardwalk, two citizens— WHITE citizens—offered Clyde friendly smiles and greetings. Red Horse, Arizona, he mused, you just may be my new home.

Back at the marshalls office Clyde unlocked Billy's cell. "C'mon out an' eat your supper at my desk, Billy!" he offered. "The lady at the Shoo-Fly made you a nice supper and sent us each a nice big chunk of pie for dessert! I'll get us each a mug of coffee."

Billy took the visitor's chair across from Clyde. "I'm obliged, Deputy," he said slowly. "'Specially after I was such a jerk this mornin' when I was drunk. Will you accept my apology?"

Clyde shook the offered hand without hesitation. "Billy, I'm about the last man I know to say somethin' about doin' stupid things while drunk. Last couple of years, seems like that's been my specialty. Although just lately now I AM tryin' to turn over a new leaf."

"Well, I wish you luck, deputy," said Billy sincerely. He ate in silence for a while, then looked up. "You know..." he shook his head, "a few of us cowboys were hangin' out by the fire one night, and somebody had a quart of Who Hit John, and we's passin' it around, chattin', tellin' stories, drinkin'...well, YOU know." Clyde nodded. He did indeed know. In fact he could almost feel the cheap rotgut whiskey hitting the back of his throat, making all the pain go away, the flames flickering, the easy conversation...

"So, anyway," Billy continued, "we're more'n half drunk and almost out of booze and somebody says, "Hey, let's go stand up the stage! We'll get some drinkin' money, nobody'll get hurt, it'll be fun!"

"Fun until we got our twenty six dollars and drank it up an' then sobered up to find that four drunk ass cowboys had somehow become a outlaw gang worth a hundred bucks each!" He sat in silent thought for a while. "Maybe this is my time to turn over a new leaf, too, Deputy," he said finally. "I'll do whatever time I gotta do for the stagecoach robbery and when I get out, no more drinkin'! No more stupid stunts with my stupid friends!"

Clyde held up his coffee mug in a toast. "To new beginnings!" he said. Billy smiled and clinked mugs. "To new beginnings!"

Billy was thoughtful for a while. "Clyde?" "Yes Billy?"

"You know I couldn't have shot you this morning, right?"

"Well, I'd like to think you couldn't, anyway," replied Clyde.

"No..I mean..that gun's got a broken firing pin. Can't shoot anybody. Figgered I'd better let you know, if you're gonna be wearin' it an' all."

CHAPTER FOUR

EANWHILE, DEPUTY JOSHUA Fallon was delighted to find that he and Miss Genevieve Jackson—Anomaly Jane, as he referred to her—had the stagecoach all to themselves. Miss Genevieve's feelings on the matter were somewhat more restrained. "On my way to Globe to testify in a murder case," the young marshall ventured. "Are you stopping there too?"

The beautiful young blonde nodded. "They have a man in custody there...might be someone I've been looking for." her eyes were far away.Up until then, Fallon had thought of Genevieve merely as a very pretty young lady. But when he saw the look in her eyes, he thanked God he wasn't the man she was looking for. He suspected that man was going to be having a very rough time of things in the near future.

Anomaly Jane, or Genevieve, was lost in the past, a time when the ten-year old was mostly known as Genny. Growing up in the Big Thicket country of East Texas.

It was the very end of the Civil War. At Appomattox, Lee had surrendered, handed his sword to that stuffed shirt Custer, for God's sake! Some Confederates, refusing to give up, rode to Mexico to fight with Emperor Maximilian.

Some, guerrilla trash like rode with Quantrill and Bloody Bill Anderson, took off for western lands, raiding isolated ranches and farms as they went.

At ten years old, Genny considered herself too grown-up to be taking her baths in the battered old tub they dragged into the kitchen on bath day. A young girl—a young LADY—she reminded herself—needs her privacy.

So this particular Saturday afternoon young Genny took some home-made lye soap and a towel and went off to the creek for a private bath.

But then horror erupted.

First, the gunshots. Enough that even a ten-year old knew this wasn't someone hunting, or a drunken cowhand or trapper celebrating.

This was death.

By the time Miss Genny had scrambled out of the creek and into her clothes, a plume of smoke was rising from the direction of the cabin. Not woodstove smoke or campfire smoke, either, but more like house-burning-down-smoke.

Ten-year-old Genny, crying her eyes out, managed to drag her mother's body away from the cabin to a safe place where she could bury her later. But by the time she got back to the cabin, the heat was too great and she couldn't get in to get her father.

Giving up, she went to the barn to check on the four horses. As she expected, all four had been stolen.

Hanging from a post in the barn she found her father's gunbelt and Smith and Wesson .44. He often left it there when he was feeding the horses or working around the stable. The thieves, in a hurry, must not have seen it dangling there amidst all the ropes, bridles, and assorted tack. It was too big for a ten-year old girl to wear so she carried the belt, with the pistol holstered, in one hand as she left the barn.

She carried a shovel in the other.

Genevieve had managed to half drag and half carry her mother to the tiny graveyard which already held her grandma and a baby sister who'd been stillborn. She had wrapped the body in a patchwork quilt as neatly as she could and begun digging. By the time big Buck Hardin, accompanied by a couple of his sons (he had four, every one tougher than rawhide) and a visiting sixteen-year old nephew, galloped up, she had a good sized grave half dug. The Hardins, the Jacksons' nearest neighbors, had been drawn by the smoke.

The four men sat their lathered horses in silence for a minute. "Yore mom?" inquired Buck finally, gesturing toward the quilt-wrapped bundle. "Yes, sir," answered Genevieve quietly. "I won't be able to get my father until the cabin cools down some."

Heavily, Buck got down from his horse. "I'm mighty sorry about yore parents, Genny." He gently took the shovel from her hands. "Be obliged if you'd let me dig some, as a mark of respect to yore folks."

Genny collapsed more than sat to take a rest. Buck's nephew Johnny, an observant young man, saw that her hands had blistered and that the blisters had broken and bled, yet the young girl had still been digging when they rode up. "No quit in this youngster!" he marveled to himself. He also noted with wry amusement that the spot she'd chosen to sit was within arm's reach of a holstered Smith and Wesson, the gunbelt looped over a branch stub. Dismounting, Johnny took his canteen off the saddle horn and gave it to the young girl. "Take a good drink and use the rest to clean up your hands a bit," he advised. "I'm going to scout around, see if I can learn anything from the tracks."

Buck nodded his assent. "I'd say 'Be careful' but it's anyone who faces you with a gun that needs to be careful! Just remember boy, no matter how good you are, somebody low enough to do something like this would shoot you in the back from cover like an Indian, given the chance."

"Reckon I'll have to make sure they don't get one, then," grinned the cocky youngster.

Buck and his sons finished digging the grave, making it big enough for the Jacksons to be buried together. By then the cabin, though still smoking in spots, had cooled enough for Buck to go in with a square of canvas and bring Abe Jackson out. He would have nightmares about that job for months.

They buried Abe and Melinda together. Buck's son Joey had made a cross from some wood he'd found in the barn. Buck said a few words and Genny put some flowers on the grave that she'd picked. Buck told her he believed her mom 'specially would like that.

The little girl didn't cry at all the whole time. She barely spoke.

When Buck told her she'd be coming to live with his

family until they could contact her aunt in New York and decide what to do, she didn't say anything for a minute.

Then she turned to Johnny, (who'd come back and had a whispered conference with Buck) and pointed at his tied-down pistol. "Will you teach me to shoot?" the little girl asked quietly.

The young man looked down at her, bemused. Ten was way too young. And he had some troubles of his own. He needed to be movin' on soon. But after the day Genevieve Jackson had gone through, he just did not have the heart to refuse her.

"Why, sure, honey," said John Wesley Hardin gently. "I'll teach you everything you need to know about how to use a gun."

"All right then," she nodded. "I'll go."

CHAPTER FIVE

GENEVIEVE STAYED AT the Hardin ranch for three months. Then her aunt Sophie came and took her back to New York. During the three months she was at the ranch, Johnny stayed true to his word and came by every day or two and taught the little girl to shoot her father's Smith and Wesson .44 cap-and-ball revolver. The gun was way too big for her and he offered to find her a smaller one but Genny was stubborn as a Missouri mule and refused. With much practice, she became stronger and learned quickly. Johnny taught her how to take apart and clean her pistol and how to load. He told her those revolvers took so long to load that many soldiers kept spare loaded cylinders. It was faster to swap out the cylinder than to load.

After the basics, he taught her shooting at targets and then drawing and shooting. She asked him a million questions and never failed to surprise him.

"The border shift?" he laughed one day. "Where would a nine-year old-"

"I'm ten!" she interrupted. He knew that but couldn't resist teasing her.

"Okay, where would a ten-year old hear about the border shift?"

"I read about it in a book by Colonel Edward Zane Carrol Judson," Genny replied primly.

Johnny hooted with laughter. "You mean 'Ned Buntline'?" he scoffed. "Sure, you can take HIS word to the bank." But he showed her how to do the border shift anyhow.

The stagecoach slowing to a stop brought Genevieve from her memories of the past. She smiled, thinking of Johnny and all she'd learned from him.

"This is it for me," said Deputy Fallon as he got up to leave. "Be seeing you."

"Bye, Josh," she smiled at him. "And thanks for giving my friend a try as your jailer."

"My pleasure."

As the stagecoach resumed its journey, Genevieve settled into a corner seat and resumed thinking about the past...

When she arrived at the Hardin ranch, Aunt Sophie had been horrified to see the ten-year old girl out back of the ranch house at the target range the cowboys had built with hay bales for backstops and bottles and cans for targets. She would have been more horrified to learn the pistol Genevieve had been using hadn't, as she assumed, been borrowed from one of the cowhands but belonged to the tiny blonde herself. For her part, Genny was ten, but she wasn't stupid. After she cleaned and reloaded the Smith and Wesson, she hid it away in the luggage going with them to New York and her aunt never knew she had it.

Genevieve spent the next six years with Aunt Sophie and Uncle Bill. Having no children of their own, they were delighted with their new daughter, although saddened by the circumstances.

Genevieve—never Gen or Genny, for some reason—grew up a very quiet child. She was affectionate enough but somewhat distant. She did well in school but at first had no friends.

Aunt Sophie had a live-in housekeeper who was Chinese. She had a son about Genevieve's age named Peng Lee, who was still in China. When Genevieve was eleven, Po managed to bring Peng Lee to America, and soon the two children were inseparable. Genevieve taught Peng Lee to shoot using the air rifles which were all they were allowed. He taught her all the karate he knew and then attended classes with her once he found them a good teacher. Her aunt and uncle were happy to pay although to be honest it's possible they thought "karate" meant "gymnasium" in Chinese. They kept up their lessons right up until Genevieve turned eighteen and went back to Texas...

CHAPTER SIX

CLYDE LIT THE kerosene lamp on the desk. The sun sets fast in Arizona, he mused, throwing the dead match in the cold woodstove. "I'll be back in a little while with our suppers, Billy,' he promised, turning to the front door of the jail.

"Will you see if there's pie, Clyde?" Billy's voice from the cell was so hopeful that Clyde couldn't help but chuckle. "I'll see what I can do."

He opened the door and took half a step outside when a fist came out of the darkness and hit him on the side of the head. The keyring flew out of his hand as he went down to his knees and rough hands grabbed his collar and threw him out onto the dusty street. He could barely see the two men in the dim light but he was pretty sure he didn't know either one. Then one of them grunted a word he recognized and he realized he'd known them his whole life. His gun was on the ground eight feet away—too far.

When you have no chance to win or escape, the only thing left to do is go down fighting. Clyde attacked the two strangers. He hit the one on the left a vicious right cross but the one on the right nailed him in the breadbasket and he went down to his knees again, head still ringing from the first sucker punch,and gasping for breath from this last shot. The man drew his pistol and clubbed Clyde across the head with the butt, then reversed it and took aim. As Clyde passed out, he heard the gunshot and thought, "Well, at least I'll get to see my family again."

Then blackness.

———

Genevieve had come to Globe to look at a prisoner in custody there. She was hoping it was a man named Burdette, but the man sitting quietly in the cell was much too young to be him.She'd been chasing him since shortly after she'd turned eighteen...

Ten-year old Genevieve had nightmares about that horrible afternoon she lost her family almost every night for months and months. Eventually she got much better although the bad dreams never went away completely. But one night a few weeks after her eighteenth birthday, she had a different kind of dream about The Day. In it, she remembered something she had completely forgotten for all these years, remembered it as vividly as if it had just happened. Johnny had gone looking for tracks and he had come back right as they had finished filling in the grave and she had been busy making sure the flowers she had picked were arranged just right so she wasn't really paying attention and she had forgotten right away. But now she remembered: Johnny had come back and pulled Uncle Buck aside even before taking care of his horse, an unforgivable sin among Texas cowboys. The two had talked for a little while and Johnny had taken a wallet out of his pocket and removed some papers from it. He showed them to Uncle Buck, then put them back in the wallet and gave it to Buck, who put it in his own pocket.

The dream ended there and Genevieve awoke sitting bolt upright in bed.

Uncle Buck knew who killed her parents and burned their home.

She wouldn't be given the nickname for three more years—she never wanted it anyway—but that was the night Anomaly Jane was born.

CHAPTER SEVEN

CLYDE WOKE UP lying on his back on the bunk in the jail cell which had been Billy's. His head ached like the worst hangover imaginable times ten. He tried to sit up a little bit and his head hurt so much he let out a little groan. Instantly he heard steps coming and he was surprised to see a smiling Billy himself throw open the unlocked cell door and rush inside. "Clyde!" he exclaimed happily. "I'm glad you're finally awake! How're ya feelin'? Ya want some water?"

Clyde accepted the water immediately but his fuzzy brain had to think a while about Billy's other statements. "How'm I feelin'? 'Bout like I got shot in the head, I guess... what you mean FINALLY awake? I see the lantern's lit so it's still nighttime. How long was I out?"

"Well, that fella decided to see how hard yore head is on Saturday night. It's still nighttime, alright, but it's Tuesday."

"Serious?" Clyde marveled. "I been unconscious for three days. Mighty lucky I ain't dead." He drank a little more water and lay quietly for a while.

"Now that I think about it, why AREN'T I dead? How come I'm in jail and you're out? What happened to those fellas that were tap-dancing on my noggin?" He thought for a minute. "I'm prob'ly gonna have a lot more questions but those are the only ones I can think of right now."

"Let's see," Billy mused, "you were goin' to the Shoo-Fly to get us some supper and when you opened the front door two fellas ambushed you for bein' the wrong color. They was beatin' the holy hell out of you when I saw the keys on the floor right in front of my cell! They must have flown out of your hand when you took that first punch to the face.

"I let myself out of the cell and grabbed a Winchester from the rack on the wall. Then I went outside and, uh—" he hesitated. "Well, I shot one of 'em."

"You SHOT one?"

"Yessir I did. It looked like he was gonna shoot you but a bullet in the leg changed his mind. Then I locked the two of them up, dragged you in and got you on this bunk, and went for the Doc. He took a couple of stitches in your head and said he thought you'd be fine."

"Why didn't you run away? You coulda had a three day head start by now!"

"I thought about it, Clyde. But somebody needed to take care of you and make sure the prisoners got fed. Didn't see nobody else likely to do it."

"I got to rest some now, Billy," sighed Clyde. "I sure am obliged to you for everything."

"My pleasure, Clyde."

At loose ends since the prisoner in Globe turned out not to be Burdette, Genevieve spent a couple of days relaxing at the hotel and then decided to take the two-day stage ride back to Red Horse and see how Clyde was doing. She rolled her eyes but said nothing when she found out Deputy Josh Fallon would be travelling on the same stage. It turned out he hadn't been needed to testify; the prisoner had hung himself in his cell the night before trial was to start.

Back in Red Horse, Clyde was relaxing behind the marshall's desk, sipping some coffee.It was getting on to supper time, and the jailhouse was filling with shadows.

Soon he'd have to get up and light the coal-oil lantern, but he was feeling lazy and didn't want to move just yet. He had been hearing a small scratching noise from under the desk for a minute or two before he decided to get up and have a look. He expected to find a field mouse that had gotten in, but instead there was a tiny calico kitten under there, vainly trying to get some food from a very small— and very empty bowl. "Well, hello, there, little fella. You looks to be hungry." The kitten mewed in agreement, and began happily eating a little bit of jerky Clyde shaved up for it with his knife. "Not many folks breaks INTO jail, you know," Clyde told the kitten. The kitten was too busy eating to respond.

Clyde stood musing, staring at the kitten, lost in memories. Clyde Junior, with a calico kitten Clyde had gotten him from a neighbor, Junior and the kitten playing with string, Junior napping in a sunny spot with the loudly purring kitten curled up on his chest...

Billy woke up from a nap and came to the door of his cell. Clyde was sitting at the desk in the dimly lit jailhouse office, only one candle going. The kitten was curled up on his lap sound asleep. Billy saw that Clyde's eyes looked glassy and he began to worry about his friend.

Had Clyde been drinking? Or...crying? "Clyde, are you all right?" Billy asked anxiously..

"I'se fine, Billy," Clyde smiled at his friend, although it was a poor attempt. There was silence for a while."My boy, Clyde Junior.." Clyde finally ventured, "he had hisself a kitten I got him, looked just like this one."

There was another long silence.

"For a long time, Billy..." Clyde mused, "All the good things I used to have, my wife, my little boy, our homestead, even our cat—" he grinned down at the sleeping kitten, "was buried under so much pain.." he shook his head. "That's why I drank, you know, to try an' dull the pain. I never even liked the stuff—hated the taste.

"I don't know how to explain it. My little partner here brought up some memories an' I jus' been walkin' around in my past, you know, inside my head, like. It's-it's kinda nice bein' able to remember some of the good times and not just the loss."

Billy stood for a moment staring at Clyde and the tiny kitten, trying to work out everything Clyde had said. The kitten half-opened one eye, looked back at him for a minute, and closed it again. Billy dug into the sack he had brought back from the Shoo-Fly. "If you're Clyde's partner, that make's you my partner too," he declared solemnly. "An' partners take care of each other."

Billy unwrapped a beef sandwich and took off a good

chunk of meat, which he began mincing into the bowl with his pocket knife. By now the kitten was wide awake and showing great interest in the proceedings. "You eat this up," Billy told the kitten. "You're way too skinny."

The kitten attacked the beef like a mountain lion jumping a bighorn sheep.. Billy and Clyde both burst into laughter at the tiny kitten's ferocity. "Our new partner's a savage, Billy." Clyde laughed. He ain't but a Little Bit, but he's tough!" And that's how Little Bit got named.

Billy, Mister Newton, and the calico kitten were all relaxing in the marshalls office drinking coffee. Or a saucer of milk, in the kitten's case. Suddenly everyone perked up as they heard the unmistakable sound of the stagecoach coming in at a full gallop, bypassing the stage station to come sliding to a halt in a cloud of dust in front of the marshalls office. "This can't be anything good," grumped Clyde as he stood up and slung his gunbelt around his waist. The belt only held his fighting knife and Billy's useless pistol, but at least it LOOKED impressive. Billy and Mister Newton followed him outside. The kitten thought about it, then resumed drinking it's milk.

As Clyde and his entourage stepped down off the roofed boardwalk, the stagecoach driver, a grizzled old-timer whose name Clyde didn't remember offhand, came hustling around the front of his lathered team. "Big trouble, Deputy!" he squalled. "Marshall Fallon saw a suspicious campfire and him and Miss Genevieve went to investigate and gunfire broke loose and I waited but neither of them made it back and so I ran for help—I—"here he broke down crying. "I ran away!" he sobbed.

Clyde spoke gently but firmly. "You did the right thing. Now we know what happened and can make plans accordingly."

CHAPTER EIGHT

I T HAD BEEN Josh who, glancing idly out the window at the blackness of the Arizona night, had spotted the campfire. The stage trail at that point ran along the top of an arroyo, and the fire was halfway down the arroyo on the opposite side.

Marshall Fallon banged on the roof of the stagecoach a couple of times to get the jehu's attention, then yelled, "Pull 'er over, Dave! There's something fishy here!"

As Dave was stopping the team, Fallon explained to Genevieve, "Over where that fire is was an abandoned camp for rustlers. A broken-down cabin but some very good corrals. I'm wonderin' who'd be camping there nowadays..I'm going to go take a quiet look."

"I'll go with you," responded Genevieve.

Dave was instructed to wait with the horses and stay quiet. If Josh and Genevieve didn't come back or he heard gunfire he was to move on to Red Horse and notify Clyde.

Sure enough, after ten minutes or so, Dave heard some gunfire. He waited ten minutes more in case Josh or Genevieve made it back, then he shook out his reins and lit a shuck for Red Horse.

Once Clyde heard Dave's story, he moved to the rifle rack, took down a Winchester, and began loading it. "I'm going to need you to watch the prisoners, Billy," he told him. "I'll go see what can be done for Miss Genevieve and the deputy."

After leaving the stagecoach, Deputy Fallon and Genevieve checked their weapons, waited for their eyes to adjust to the darkness, and began quietly creeping down the side of the arroyo until they got near the fire. Here Josh stopped. "You best wait here while I sneak closer. I move like a cat at night!" he boasted.

"They'll never hear me URKK!" he grunted as a rock turned under his foot and he fell, tumbling down the arroyo to end up near the fire with four dimly-seen men aiming weapons at his face.

Halfway up the arroyo wall, Genevieve rolled her eyes. "Idiot," she whispered. Four armed men holding him prisoner. How was she going to rescue him?

CHAPTER NINE

THE FOUR OUTLAWS had built their fire outside the old abandoned rustlers' cabin because the roof had fallen in over the years. The corrals behind the cabin were still stout, though, which was why the four had chosen the place. Right now there were fifteen horses penned up—horses whose brands would tell a very interesting story to any lawman who saw them.

This is why the outlaws didn't hesitate when Fallon tumbled into their midst. One of the the four, a tall man with greasy hair and burnside whiskers, took a long step forward and clouted the deputy on the side of the head with the butt of his Henry rifle. Josh went down and didn't move. Watching from the darkness, Genevieve worried that he might be dead. But then they tied his hands behind his back, so he must still be alive.

Outnumbered four to one and with only her father's .44 and her hideout Derringer against at least two rifles—maybe four!—and several handguns, Genevieve decided her only chance was to wait, to watch, and to hope for an opportunity. Her teacher in New York used to say, "look for the enemy's weakness, then attack!

There is always a way to attack, one must only find it...” Sometimes easier said than done.

After a while, three of the men went to their bedrolls around the fire while the fourth sat on a stump nearby, smoking a pipe and gazing into the flames. Genevieve knew if she made a move, the guard would have no night vision for several minutes. Experienced fighters never stared into a campfire like that.

Unfortunately Josh was right in the middle of the other three, giving her no chance. She settled down for a long wait.

Right before dawn, as the sky was just barely beginning to lighten, Genevieve made her move. The guard’s head had been nodding for a while now, he was practically asleep sitting up. Genevieve crept down the side of the arroyo as stealthily as a prowling mountain lion. She paused near the semi-sleeping guard long enough to apply a Chinese choke hold which would keep him unconscious for a while. Easing him gently and quietly to the ground, Genevieve worked her way into the middle of the three sleeping outlaws. Attempting to wake Fallon quietly, she put a hand over his mouth as she quietly whispered his name in his ear.

That’s when everything fell apart. Fallon woke up thrashing his arms and by the time he stopped all three outlaws were awake and had pistols aimed at the duo.

“Looks like our prisoner got himself a friend!” one of them cackled. This one was missing half his teeth and hadn’t had a bath since the last rainstorm.

"A pretty one, too!" chimed in the one closest to Genevieve. He had even less teeth than the first and, from the smell, must have taken shelter somewhere during that last rainstorm. He leered at her menacingly. "I think we oughtta strip 'er down an'—"

He was interrupted by the flat crack of a Winchester. Fired from the darkness somewhere up the arroyo, the bullet took him dead center chest and he dropped instantly, dead before he hit the ground. Unfortunately, the chief if the outlaws, a man named Bannon, thought very quickly and jumped behind Genevieve so she was shielding him from the unknown rifleman. He told her, "Don't you make a move or my partner will drill yore friend right through his noggin!" He had the barrel of his pistol pressed firmly against the base of Genevieve's skull when he raised his voice and called out in the general direction of where the shot had come from. "Here's how it is, friend!" he yelled. "If you don't throw down yore gun and come out where we can see yuh by the time I count three, I'm gonna shoot this little lady in the head and dive for cover. You might get me or you might not, but either way this lady's dead. One....two—"

"All right, all right!" said a disgusted voice from the darkness, and Clyde came walking towards the camp. He had his hands half-raised and his pistol holster and knife sheath were both empty. He had left the rifle and pistol behind but the knife was behind his belt in the back where nobody could see it. He stopped about fifteen feet away from the little circle of outlaws—one dead, one unconscious, and two holding guns—and their captives. "Hello,

Miss Genevieve," he said. "Hello, Clyde!" Genevieve spoke brightly. "I really like your new clothes."It was starting to become lighter out although the sun hadn't risen yet.

Light enough the horse thieves—the live and conscious ones, anyway—could see the badge on Clyde's shirt. "More law, Bannon!" said the dentally-and olfactorily-challenged outlaw disgustedly. "I reckon we've used this hideout for the last time."

Bannon nodded. "Keep an eye on these three,Tote," he ordered. He holstered his Remington .44. He threw some wood on the campfire from the stack nearby and put on the kettle for coffee once the fire was blazing brightly. "So here's the plan," he said finally. "We'll have some coffee and pack up camp.

Even with just the two of us (he was assuming Genevieve had killed the lookout she'd knocked unconscious since that's what he would have done) we can get those horses to where we're meetin' up with Barlow. Once we got our money, we'll head for New Mexico and relax for a while. I got some friends there."

"Awright," his sole remaining gang member, Tote, seemed doubtful. "But what about these two lawmen and their girlfriend? You know as well as I do what happens if you harm a woman out here on the frontier! The law won't EVER stop huntin' us! Not until we're hangin' from a scaffold!"

"I know it," agreed Bannon. "Maybe we can—"

Whatever plan he had come up with went undisclosed, however. Both outlaws were suddenly startled when the third member of the gang—who they had both thought was dead!—suddenly jerked to a sitting position, shouting something unintelligible. Tote, in fact, was so startled that he made a fatal mistake: he spun around to look, so his gun was no longer aimed at the deputy. It was the last mistake he ever made because instantly the unmistakable BOOM of a Sharps Big Fifty roared from up the arroyo and most of his head disappeared in a red mist.

Bannon, no doubt planning to try the hostage trick with Genevieve again, went for his Remington. He was very fast, but he barely had the gun clear of its' holster when there was the spiteful crack of a Derringer which had miraculously appeared in Genevieve's hand, and he sagged, but kept trying to get the suddenly-heavy revolver on target Genevieve was forced to fire the Derringer's second shot into him, leaving it empty.

The lookout Genevieve had choked out was now the only one remaining alive. He'd awakened in the middle of a gunfight and had no idea what was going on but he recognized Genevieve as an enemy when she shot his boss.

He started to line up a shot on the now-unarmed young woman but he was only about eighteen feet away from Clyde and that was way too close for the old Buffalo Soldier to miss. He drew the fighting knife from behind his back smoothly and threw it forcefully. The knife turned end-over-end once and took the outlaw in the throat. He was dead although it took a couple of minutes for his body to catch up and realize the idea.

All four outlaws were dead. Clyde and Genevieve were unharmed.

Deputy Fallon was still floating between conscious and not-conscious from the rifle butt to the head.

"Do you know who that is behind the Sharps rifle, Clyde?" inquired Genevieve as the two of them checked the dead and policed up the loose weapons.

"Yes, ma'am," Clyde replied miserably. "Do you remember that young fella Billy that I'se supposed to be keeping safely locked up in the jail?"

"Ye-es?"

"Well, I s'pect that's him."

CHAPTER TEN

B Y THE TIME full daylight had arrived, Clyde and Genevieve had put out the campfire, gathered up all the weapons, and loaded the four outlaw corpses on four horses they chose from the corral. They had also saddled horses for the three of them, although whether the still-groggy deputy would be able to sit a horse was questionable. The rest of the outlaws' gear and the remaining horses in the corral would be left until someone could come out from Red Horse to collect them.

As expected, Clyde and Genevieve topped out of the arroyo only to find Billy waiting for them, Deputy Fallon's Sharps scabbarded at his side and a sheepish grin on his face. "H'lo, Clyde, ma'am," he said. "I'm glad yore both alright."

"Thanks to YOU, Billy," Clyde replied.

Genevieve looked confused. "When we get back to Red Horse, the two of you are going to have quite a bit of explaining to do," she told them.

"I know it's confusing, Miss Genevieve," Clyde told her. "But I promise, I'll explain everything when we get back to Red Horse."

"There's a lot to tell," mused Billy. "How the rednecks tried to kill Clyde and I shot one and Clyde was unconscious for three days and the kitten adopted us and the stagecoach came in without you and—"

"Easy, partner," chuckled Clyde. "We'll tell her and the deputy the whole story…"

It was around noontime and one hundred and five degrees when their little group entered Red Horse. The half-unconscious deputy, the pretty blonde, and their black-and-white companions, would have gathered some attention even without the four corpse-carrying horses they were leading.

By the time they neared the marshalls office and jail, Mister Newton was waiting outside with his stablehand. "We'll take care of these horses after we bring the bodies to the undertaker," he told the weary travellers. Soon, Clyde, Genevieve, Josh, and Billy had trooped into the office. Josh collapsed behind his desk while Genevieve and Clyde took the two rickety visitors' chairs and Billy began heating up some coffee.

After mugs of the steaming brew had been passed all around, Clyde looked at the deputy, still pale and somewhat groggy, and ventured, "Deputy, there's some medicine in the bottom drawer there if you think it might help."

Fallon took a flat pint of whiskey from the drawer. He opened it and put a healthy slug in his coffee, which he then sipped with evident satisfaction. "That bottle was still sealed," he observed.

"Why, yessir it is," replied Clyde. "I promised you I wouldn't drink while I was your jailer, and I intended to try hard to keep my word, but then these fellas knocked me unconscious and I didn't wake up for three days. I guess by then any withdrawal problems had worked its way through me...I been so busy since then I don't even really think about liquor at all anymore."

But of course then he had to tell them the story of the rednecks knocking him unconscious and Billy shooting one of them and arresting all of them even though he was technically a prisoner himself. After locking them up, Billy had dragged the unconscious Clyde into a cell and then brought the doctor, a notorious racist, to the jail at gunpoint and watched him like a hawk while he stitched Clyde up.

"Course, that don't explain what my prisoner was doin' back in the brush with your Sharps rifle," Clyde observed, "but since we woulda' been in quite the fix without him, I don't b'lieve I'll give him a hard time about it."

Billy looked sheepish. "I'm sorry for borrowin' your rifle without askin', Deputy."

Fallon waved him off. "No problem. We were lucky you followed along."

Genevieve echoed the mens' thanks, but it could be easily seen that she was depressed. "You seem mighty sad, Miss Genevieve," Clyde noted kindly. "May I ask what's botherin' you? Maybe I could help."

Genevieve smiled a little sadly. "I'm just a little disappointed, Clyde," she responded. "I've been trying to catch this man for a long time." Her voice was forlorn. "When I was a little girl, four men robbed and killed my parents. I was down at the creek. If they'd known I was there they would have killed me too. They stole all the horses and burned the house and barn. My aunt took me in and I grew up in New York City."

"Is that why you became a bounty hunter, Miss Genevieve?" Billy was on the edge of his seat. Easily led and a little slow in his thinking, Billy was basically kind-hearted and the story of the little girl orphaned so violently horrified him. "So you can make them four scum pay for what they did?"

"Pretty much, Billy," she agreed. "Although there are only two of them left, now. My neighbor Johnny followed them for a ways and got close enough to shoot one before the rest of them escaped. From the papers on the body, we figured out who the other three were. I shot and killed one of them two years ago. I was willing to arrest him even after what he'd done, but he started shooting and left me no choice. The other two..." she shrugged helplessly. "Maybe we'll cross paths someday."

There was silence for a while. The four unlikely friends sipped their coffee and relaxed. It was nice not to have anyone shooting at you for a while.

The calico kitten, sensing Genevieve's sadness—cats have a special sense which allows them to do that—strolled across the desktop to the lady. Then it plopped down into her lap and began happily kneading biscuits with her front paws, purringly louder than a steam engine until Genevieve could not help but smile. Chinscratching made the purring even louder.

Watching Genevieve with the kitten, seeing how the

little scamp had cheered up their friend, all three men independently resolved to get L'il Bit a special treat at the general store tomorrow.

"What's your friend's name?" Genevieve inquired, chuckling as the little calico head-butted her hand to demand more chin scratching.

"We call him L'il Bit," Billy told her. "He sort of adopted us."

Genevieve rolled her eyes. "Men!" she teased them, pretending to be scornful. "Don't you know a lady when you see one?" Seeing their confusion, she told them, "L'il Bit is a girl." She was so certain that noone questioned her.

Billy was dumbfounded but, shy with women, was afraid to ask her how she knew. Clyde, however, rose to the occasion. "Don't matter none if she's a she or a he, Miss Genevieve. She's still a part of this happy little tribe we got goin' here.

We got us a stalwart defender of law and order"—he nodded at Josh, who saluted him with his whiskey-laced coffee before taking a sip—"a beat-up old ex-drunk Buffalo Soldier turned jailer, a wanted-poster, sixgun slingin' stagecoach robber determined to reform (Billy blushed red but stayed quiet) a beautiful lady bounty hunter on a quest for revenge, and their feisty calico kitten mascot.

Mister Ned Buntline could easily write one of those "penny dreadful" novels about us!"

Miss Genevieve chuckled. "Is there any more coffee?" she asked, handing Clyde her mug when he gestured for it. "Thanks." She took a sip and smiled at him. "You make much better coffee than I do, Clyde. I'll tell you boys a story about Colonel Edward Carrol Zane Judson, if you'd like."

"Who's that Colonel Judson fella, Miss Genevieve?" asked Billy.

"Colonel Edward Zane Carrol Judson is supposedly the name of the author who goes by the pen name of Ned Buntline, Billy," Genevieve told him. "Although I'm positive he stole title of "Colonel" and I would not be surprised if the rest of his name was bogus too.

"Anyway, he came to see me in Kansas after I apprehended "One Gun" Thompson. He was supposed to be fast but it turned out One Gun wasn't enough. I sent him off to prison with a slightly perforated shoulder and Ned Buntline took me to dinner.

He told me lady bounty hunters were extremely rare and beautiful ones almost nonexistent. He called me an Anomaly and said it meant something unique and one-of-a-kind. He wanted to write a series of books about me and call them "The Lady Gunslinger" books." She paused, lost in thought.

"Did you let him write them books?" Billy asked. "Is that why folks call you Anomaly Jane?"

Genevieve smiled at his childlike enthusiasm for the story. "I refused to work with him on the books once I found out what a lying weasel he was. He did write one but it was all lies and sensationalism.

"But anyway—here's what happened. The noted author, Ned Buntline, rented a large tent and charged people two dollars a head to come listen to him lecture on the Benefits of Temperance and the Evils of Alcohol. I bet there were a hundred and fifty people crammed in there.

"Mister Buntline stood at one end of the tent, a portly man with mutton chop whiskers. In front of him was a podium on top of which were some handwritten notes, a pitcher of ice water, and a glass. As he began speaking in a clear, carrying baritone, he poured himself a glass of water and would occassionally pause to take a sip, the day being warm.

"Oh, he was a talker, all right! He told stories of hardworking men who had lost jobs and families to alcohol, soldiers and sailors who had been responsible for untold deaths of their teammates due to being too drunk too fulfill their duties, and much more. His entire audience was moved.

"But...as he continued to tell his stories and sip his water, his elocution became less crisp. In fact he almost seemed to be slurring his words a little. And I was fairly certain he was about to begin a story about an English sailor for the third time when two of his friends, who had been seated very close to the front, climbed on stage and unceremoniously removed Mister Buntline from the premises. As the audience sat perplexed, wondering what had happened, if the show was over, and what to do, a small wiry man from the front row climbed up on the stage. He lifted the ice-water pitcher, sniffed the contents, then stuck a finger inside. He licked his finger, grimaced, and announced disgustedly, "It's gin!" Mister Buntline is lucky he escaped lynching that day." The three men chuckled at her story.

Deputy Fallon had mostly been sitting quiet. Other than forgiving Billy for absquatulating with his Sharps rifle, and thanking both Billy and Clyde for their help, he hadn't said much, mostly due to his rifle-butt induced throbbing head-ache. But the whiskey and the coffee and the quiet chatter of his friends had him feeling much more like his old self.

"Now that I understand your distaste for the name, I will call you Miss Genevieve and no longer Anomaly Jane," he ventured. "And to make amends for my indiscretions, I also have a good nickname story to share." Clyde, Billy and Genevieve waited expectantly for the story. L'il Bit did not, since she had fallen sound asleep on Genevieve's lap.

"Well," began the deputy, "down in the cow towns, they got themselves a gunslingin' marshall named James Butler Hickock. He's a long-haired, bearded dandy who wears twin revolvers in a red sash around his waist, and he's sup-posed to be quicker than greased lightning with 'em, too."

"I've heard of him!" Billy chimed in excitedly. "They call him Wild Bill Hickock!"

"That's the man, all right," agreed the deputy. He leaned forward conspiratorially. "Now, the story I heard is that Mister Hickock is a man of, shall we say, somewhat unfor-tunate facial features, a fact he wears the beard and mus-tache to cover up. Apparently that didn't work: a boisterous gentleman in a bar nicknamed him "Duck Bill".

Mister Hickock took offense and shot the man dead, at which point the nickname became changed to "Wild Bill." Much more fitting, I think."

"I do love a story with a happy ending," Clyde said dryly.

"Except for the fella who got shot, of course." Everybody laughed.

"By the way, is there any paper out on the two renegades you're looking for?" asked the deputy. By "paper" he meant wanted posters.

"Not that I know of," Genevieve replied regretfully. "I just have their descriptions—a six-foot-seven inch giant close to four hundred pounds, none of it fat, and a medium height, black-haired man with a scar like a pitchfork on his cheek."

Clyde had been leaning back against the wall, his chair on two legs, sipping his coffee and listening. Now he brought his chair forward with a thump, his eyes narrowed. Grabbing a pencil, he took an old invoice from the clutter on the desk and turned it over to draw on the back.

He drew a three-pronged pitchfork. The middle prong extended back to become the handle. The right hand prong had a line coming back off of it at an angle like the barb on a fish hook.

"Does it look like this?" he asked quietly.

Genevieve gazed at the drawing wide-eyed. "It looks exactly like that."

"A dark-haired man, maybe Deputy Fallon's size, with that scar on his right cheek? Maybe forty years old? Bushy mustache.." he thought for a minute. "I disremember what kind of pistol he had but he carried it on the left side, butt forward."

"The mustache is new," Genevieve admitted, "but everything else is exactly right. It HAS to be Burdette!"

"He calls himself Billings now," Clyde told her. "And unless he's moved in the past year or so—which I doubt since he had a nice little ranch and plenty of fat cows—then he's less'n a two days' ride from here! I can take you right to him!"

CHAPTER ELEVEN

CLYDE AND GENEVIEVE spent the rest of the day making plans and getting ready for their journey. Josh Fallon wanted to accompany them but was overruled by the doctor, who cleaned up his head and told him he probably had a concussion and to spend a few days in bed.

Billy was heartbroken he couldn't go along to help his friends, but the deputy refused to grant him parole. He trusted Billy to come back; he just couldn't have him roaming around while those "Wanted" posters were still up. Be a helluva thing to get shot over twenty-six dollars. Clyde told Billy privately he wasn't happy about the deputy's head wound and to make sure he ate good and didn't over exert himself. Billy was happier, feeling needed once given a task.

Along with arranging for horses and purchasing some trail supplies, Clyde stopped by the gunsmith and had Billy's pistol repaired. He was still wearing it, Billy having told him to keep it as long as he wanted.

And of course he had his fighting knife on the other side. He had hung onto one of the dead outlaws' rifles, an old but well-cared for Spencer just like the one he'd carried in the cavalry, and he picked up plenty of ammunition for both weapons. And last but most important, he filled several canteens with fresh water. There was no such thing as too much water when crossing the Arizona desert.

That evening, Clyde and Genevieve walked into the Shoo-Fly Restaurant where a beaming Miss Amy (the black restaurant owner and cook who Billy insisted had a crush on Clyde) led them to her only table for six, since they had guests coming. Miss Amy kept a clean place, with white painted walls and red and white check tablecloths. There were only a few diners still in the restaurant since all had decided on a late supper.

In a few minutes Josh Fallon, accompanied by Billy, entered with smiles and greetings. No sooner had they seated themselves than Mister Newton walked in, completing the guest list. The sixth chair remained empty for now, but Miss Amy had agreed to join them for dessert if her duties allowed.

Clyde opened the proceedings while they waited for their food—there were no menus at the Shoo-Fly, you ate what they brought you, and it was always good—by saying, "I'm glad we all could get together for a meal. I haven't had this many friends since I was in the Tenth Cavalry. I want to thank Josh for lettin' Billy have the evening off from jail to see us off (the deputy, sporting a snowy white bandage on his head, smiled and made a "don't mention it" wave) and also Mister Newton for lendin' us the horses for our trip."

"My pleasure, Clyde. Just make sure the two of you stay safe, and I'll be more than pleased."

That was Newton for you, Clyde reflected. He hadn't even asked why Clyde wanted to borrow two horses and tack from the stage company. He didn't care. His friend needed horses; he had horses. That simple.

CHAPTER TWELVE

CLYDE WAS STILL thinking about the dinner party bright and early the next morning when he was saddling up. It was almost like having a family again, he mused, not by blood but by choice. Once someone had risked their lives for you, and you had done the same for them, a bond was formed which lasted forever. "You know, horse," he told the big sorrel, patting his neck and talking soothingly, "I'se in an awful good mood for a fella that's prob'ly goin' to get his black ass shot to pieces at the end of this trip. This Burdette is nobody to mess with." The horse nickered as if in agreement. He was a beauty, clean-limbed and strong. Newton had given them his best, it looked like. When she joined him at the stable, Genevieve fell in love with the little dun gelding as quickly as he did with her.

She had exchanged the dress she wore when traveling on the stage for a shirt and pants like a man. This would have been scandalous back East but was fairly common in Arizona. The pants were made of cotton or denim and, Clyde couldn't help noticing, fit snugly, and were tucked into her boots. Her father's .44 rode in a custom gunbelt and she wore the straw hat.

Clyde already had her Winchester and his Spencer is scabbards on their respective saddles. Good to go.

In no time, Genevieve and Clyde were following the well-defined stagecoach trail east. The sky was achingly beautiful, blue and cloudless. The temperature was still only in the low eighties. The landscape along the trail was mostly desert, dotted here and there with Joshua trees and the uniquely Arizonan saguaro. Occasionally there were bones, maybe buffalo, maybe cow. Once in a while human.

After an hour and a half or so, Clyde and Genevieve pulled off the trail to where a tiny creek trickled its way through the the area. No more than a foot wide and four inches deep, it was still fresh clean water and the horses enjoyed it thoroughly. Clyde left the saddles on the horses but loosened the cinches. He and Genevieve sat on the grass and relaxed while the horses grazed.

"How is it you know Mister Burdette—or Billings, as you know him by?" inquired Genevieve.

Clyde thought a while, chewing idly on a stem of grama grass.

"I guess it was about a year ago," he finally replied. "Maybe a year and a half. I met him in a saloon. Apart from a drinking place, a Western saloon is also sort of a meetinghouse, a place to find an employee if you're hirin', a job if you're lookin' or just catch up on the local gossip.

"I had just wandered into town that day. This big fella with a pitchfork scar walks up to me at the bar and growls, "I don't know you."

"I just got into town," I told him.

"We don't like strangers here," he informed me. Seeing the way my hand was hoverin' near my gun, he backed down a little bit. "Lookin' fer a job, are ya?" he inquired.

"Maybe," I replied.

He waved to the bartender for drinks. "I'll buy a round," he offered. His eyes twinkled a little. "That way I won't have to shoot you for a stranger."

He told me his name was Billings and, after another round and some conversation, offered me a cowboyin' job on his ranch, the Slash B. Thing was, I had been in town several hours and I heard a lot about this Billings fella.

"Seems he had come into the area two years earlier, having bought the old Bar 7 when the owners moved to California. He come in with a hard-bitten crew that looked more like gunslingers than cowpunchers, and about a thousand head of magic cattle.

"See, the locals figgered those cows was magic because by the followin' spring's roundup, they had each managed to have three or even four calves! Nobody did anything about it because that was a mighty gun-handy crew he had, but I decided I didn't want to work for him and kept movin' on down the road. He was makin' good money; I 'spect he's still there."

"I certainly hope so."

They continued on in silence. The temperature rose. The sun beat down unmercifully. Back in Red Horse, Billy paced back and forth in his unlocked cell, fretting about his friends. Deputy Josh Fallon, seated behind his desk, appeared calm but was inwardly tied up in knots just as bad as Billy. The calico kitten, sleeping on the floor in a ray of sunshine from the window, was the only one who was untroubled.

CHAPTER THIRTEEN

"T**HIS DON'T LOOK** good, Miss Genevieve," Clyde told the young blonde woman hunkered down in the rocks beside him. He closed his brass spyglass with a snap. "He's down there, all right, I seen that scar of his plain as day. But there's four men with guns with him in the ranch house and eight to ten more in the bunkhouse, not countin' the cook. We can't attack that many head-on. What do you think we should do?"

Genevieve shook her head, frustrated. "I think the only thing we can do is wait and watch and look for an opening."

The opening they were hoping for came early the next morning, after an uncomfortable night in the rocks taking turns napping and watching the Slash B. Billings, accompanied only by one man, rode out of the ranch yard and took the trail south.

"There's a sort of no-account town a couple miles that way," Clyde informed Genevieve. "Ain't much. A trading post, a dirty saloon with a couple of cribs out back, a livery stable...maybe a couple of shacks."

Genevieve stood up. Her eyes were like fire. "Let's go."

The man now known as Billings had started in Tenessee

as a Higgins. Billings and Burdette weren't the only names he'd borrowed in keeping clear of the law. By any name, he was trash.

Billings, after a mediocre breakfast with his hired gun Slade, stepped down off the restaurant's boardwalk into the bright sun of the street. The brilliant light made him squint so much it took him a minute to make out the young blonde woman facing him in the street.

He noted the gun hanging around her slender waist but was too arrogant to ever consider a woman a threat. "I know you?" he called.

The beautiful young woman shrugged. Out of the corner of his eye, Billings saw Slade leave the restaurant only to be immediately disarmed by a medium sized black man with a Colt revolver.

"You won't remember me!" the young woman told Billings. "In Texas, right after the War, you killed my parents, stole our horses, and burned our place to the ground."

Billings smiled. "I've killed so many, it's hard to remember specifics. Guess it's your turn, now, since I—" he went for his gun, trying to catch her by surprise.

Genevieves flashing draw was so quick that Billings only had his gun half out of the holster before she fired. It should have been over right then. Except she missed.

Unknown to Clyde and Genevieve, Billings and Slade weren't the only men in town from the Slash B. The Dexter twins had been sleeping in the stable, having come in late the night before. Dark, medium-sized, unshaven and dirty, the Dexter brothers were actually born two years apart.

Their identical appearance, their habit of dressing alike, and the fact that they were always together made the "twins" nickname inevitable.

The twins came out the open stable doors just in time to see Genevieve in front of the restaurant confronting their boss. No believer in fair play, both men drew their revolvers and opened fire. The distance was much too great for accurate revolver fire and neither man had a rifle with him, but one twin got lucky and shot Genevieve in the left shoulder just as she fired, causing her to jerk and miss her shot at Billings. He missed a shot at her as she flung herself behind a full water barrel on the sidewalk for cover.

Genevieve realized she was in a very bad spot. Billings was firing from inside the doorway of the restaurant; the twins were popping out from the corner of the stable, not trying to hit her from that range, just keep her pinned down.

Suddenly a Spencer rifle began firing steadily from up the street, and Clyde came galloping up on his sorrel, leading Genevieve's horse.

Clyde was guiding his horse with his knees like a Buffalo Soldier or a Comanche warrior, leaving his hands free to fire.

When the Spencer was first invented, it was known as "the rifle you could load on Sunday and fire all week." Clyde's held sixteen rounds in a tubular magazine and he used every round to keep Billings and the Twins' heads down. He stopped only long enough for Genevieve to leap into the saddle, then the two of them took off out of town as fast as they could go, dust billowing up behind them.

Either somebody had got to a rifle or just made one ungodly lucky shot with a revolver because a sharp stinging in his right thigh told Clyde he'd been nicked. Quite a bit of blood, maybe a little more than a nick. In front of him about ten yards, Genevieve was holding on to her saddle like a trooper, but he could see quite a bit of blood on her shirt.

Clyde held the horses to a gallop for a while, then slowed them and left the trail where a pair of cottonwoods provided some shade. He dismounted and helped Genevieve down. "We can't stay here, Miss Genevieve," he apologized. "I don't see any dust behind us, but that don't mean they ain't comin'. We'll rest up the horses a little bit while we tend to your shoulder, then we gots to be movin'."

"What do you think we should do?"

"I don't b'lieve we have a choice. Billings might be satisfied with chasin' us off, but we can't count on that. He could come after us with them three fellas from the town, or he could could send word to the ranch for men and have a dozen guns on our trail.

"And whether four guns or a dozen, we're in no shape for another fight. You need a sawbones to look at that shoulder, 'an I got a hole in my leg. It ain't bad but I don't think I'll be movin' too quick for a while.

"No, I think we gotta run. We get back to Red Horse and we'll have a safe place to heal up and decide what to do next. All right?"

Genevieve moved her arm around experimentally. She winced at the pain, and sighed. "I don't suppose we have much choice." Clyde grinned crookedly. "Well, we could go back and let Billings and his men shoot us to doll rags, if you want."

Genevieve managed a smile. Now that the adrenaline was wearing off her shoulder was really starting to throb. "Red Horse it is," she agreed. "I could really use a cup of Billy's coffee about now."

Genevieve sat while Clyde, limping pretty good, gave each of the horses a hatful of water. He made sure Genevieve kept sipping from one of her canteens, too, since she'd lost blood. He gave the horses a little grain and left them to tend to Miss Genevieve. Since the bullet had gone all the way through the shoulder, Clyde put a pad made from bandaging material they'd carried with them on both entrance and exit, winding a strip of bandage around her to keep the pads in place. "I'll clean it up good and rebandage it when we find a place to hole up later," he promised. "Doc'll have to stitch you up when we get back, but I think you'll be fine." Clyde had been fairly lucky as far as his own wound. The bullet had just barely clipped his thigh, gouging out a chunk of meat and continuing on. It hurt like hell but wasn't really serious. A bandanna tied around the leg was all the medical attention he was willing to take time for, feeling the need to get moving. If Billings and his men caught up with them now they couldn't put up much of a fight.

CHAPTER FOURTEEN

CLYDE AND GENEVIEVE got into the town of Red Horse late in the afternoon of the following day. Miss Genevieve's wound did not look to be infected, but she was flushed and running a fever. Clyde brought her directly to the doctor's office, which was on the main street next door to Brennan's Saloon. This was very convenient for the doctor, who had a great fondness for alcohol.

"You wait there a second and I'll help you down," Clyde told the girl. Dismounting, he looped both horses' reins over the hitching rail, then reached up both arms as she sagged towards him, staggering back a few steps under the unexpected weight as she pitched forward, unconscious. For the last ten miles or so, she had been keeping herself in the saddle by sheer determination and will power. Clyde picked her up and carried her into the doctor's office.

The doctor began preparing his instruments as quickly as possible. "Better if I operate now while she's already unconscious and won't feel the pain." Luckily, it was before supper and the doc was still sober, or as close as he ever got to it.

"I need to talk to the marshall and let him know Miss

Genevieve's been shot," Clyde told the doctor. "I'll be back to check on her in an hour or so."

"I'll take a look at your leg wound when you get back," the doctor offered. He said it somewhat grudgingly but Clyde was still surprised he offered at all. "Thanks, doctor," he said as he left.

Deputy Marshall Fallon was seated behind his desk in the jailhouse, playing a game of checkers with Billy. The kitten was seated on the desk, watching intently and occasionally trying to steal one of the checkers. Despite his worries about Genevieve and the pain from his leg, Clyde couldn't help but grin at the sight.

"Seems like you two was having a right nice time while me and Miss Genevieve was off gettin' shot to pieces," he said, pretending to grumble.

Billy bolted up out of the visitor's chair. "You sit right here, Clyde," he exclaimed. "Are you hurt bad? Where's Miss Genevieve? Is she hurt too?"

"Calm down a minute and let the man breathe, damnit!" ordered the deputy marshall. "We got hot coffee and there's some bear sign in that bag on the windowsill."

Clyde's eyes lit up at the mention of the pastry. "Now you talkin'! The last two days has been a worrisome time." He sat down and took a sip of the coffee Billy brought him, then crumbled a piece off the bear sign for the kitten, who was staring at him hopefully. He told the marshall and Billy about the gunfight and how it had gone wrong, with both him and Miss Genevieve wounded. "So I concluded the only thing to do was to run like a rabbit back here, where we can get doctored up and not worry too much about bein' ambushed in town. I don't think Billings and his guns would try that." There were about eighty-five men living in Red Horse at the time and most of them had fought in the War Between the States or in Indian battles coming west. All of them had rifles or shotguns—sometimes both—and kept them loaded and handy. Indian or outlaw attack was always a possibility and it only made sense to be prepared.

Josh Fallon thought a minute, then agreed. "I don't think you had any choice. Especially with Genevieve hurt and all." It was no secret that Fallon was in love with Genevieve, but she seemed to think of him as a younger brother. Maybe one that had been kicked in the head by a mule, and thus needed to be talked to slowly, and with small words.

Relaxing in his chair, with the warmth of the coffee in his belly, the calico kitten purring itself to sleep on his lap, and the knowledge that (at least for the moment) nobody was shooting at him, Clyde was almost asleep when Billy asked, "So what's the plan? How we gonna get these guys that shot you and Miss Genevieve?" Clyde cocked an eyebrow at his young friend. "We?"

"That's right!" Billy bristled. "I'm a free man now and I can go where I want!"

"Serious now Billy?"

"Yes sir. The marshall spent almost all day on the telegraph yesterday and I am free as a bird!"

Now Clyde cocked the same skeptical eyebrow at Josh, who shrugged a little sheepishly. "I told a judge I'm friendly with that in my opinion Billy wasn't so much guilty of stagecoach robbery as he was of being a dumbass who went along with his drunken friends without thinking about the consequences. I also pointed out that he had saved the lives of, first, my jailer during an attack in town, and then myself and the noted bounty hunter Anomaly Jane later. The judge sentenced Billy to "time served" and I spent the rest of the day telegraphing every marshall and sheriff in the area to throw away their paper on Billy Tyler, noted desperado."

Billy spoke up now. "So the bottom line is if you go after the outlaws that shot you and Miss Genevieve, I'm going too. If Josh will lend me his Sharps again I'll take it but if all I have is my Buck knife I'm still going!"

The deputy nodded in agreement. "I'm goin' too.My prisoners have been transported and my jail's empty. If the city council don't like it, too bad, I've got plenty of vacation time comin' to me. And, Billy, I don't own a Sharps rifle anymore. As far as I'm concerned, I gave that gun to you the night you used it to save me and Genevieve from gettin' shot in the head by them horse thieves. And besides," he blushed a little, "I gotta be honest, I never been able to hit a damn thing with it anyway. I'm good with a six-gun but that's about it. You and that gun seem like you was made for each other, somehow..."

Clyde smiled at his two friends. "I'm goin' down to the doc's to check on Miss Genevieve," he told them, "and he offered to fix up my leg, too. Once we're patched up, we'll make some plans."

"Good," said the deputy marshall. "How 'bout we all meet up later at your girlfriend's place to eat?" He was referring to Miss Amy at the Shoo-Fly Restaurant. As the only black man and black woman in Red Horse, and both being single, it was assumed that Clyde and Miss Amy would wind up together at some point. "Sounds like a plan," Clyde grinned. "See you then."

CHAPTER FIFTEEN

CLYDE HAD BEEN careful on the trip back to Red Horse as much as possible. They'd traveled on rock to avoid leaving sign when they could, and joined their tracks with those of a medium sized herd of cattle for a while before cutting off for town.

But he didn't know about Injun. Injun worked for Billings, had been with him back when his name was Burdette, in fact. He wore white man's pants and cowhide vest, high-top Comanche mocassins, and a red Apache headband. Nobody knew if he was white or Indian or some mix of both and nobody cared; Injun was just a handy nickname because of his clothes. White or Indian, he could track a snake over a flat rock. He had no trouble shadowing Clyde and Genevieve all the way back to Red Horse. He stayed far enough back that neither of them realized they were being pursued.

Twice he could have ambushed them with his Winchester and probably killed them both. But his instruction from Billings had been very clear, so Injun merely followed and watched.

Soon Billings and some of the boys would be along, and they'd decide what to do. Billings had no idea who Clyde was but he had instantly recognized Genevieve as the lady gunslinger who had given him the pitchfork scar on his face and almost killed him. He was in the worst rage Injun had ever seen him in, swearing revenge for his scar and for attacking him and his men.

Injun found a good hiding spot halfway up one of the low buttes behind Red Horse and settled in for the wait.

CHAPTER SIXTEEN

SUPPER THAT EVENING was a fairly cheerful affair considering Miss Genevieve was too shot-up to attend, Clyde and Josh were both recovering from wounds, and it was a good bet that Billings, now that he knew Genevieve was in the area, would be looking for her with blood on his mind.

Still, you take the good where you can find it. The doc said Miss Genevieve's shoulder would heal good as new, though it would be a while mending; Clyde and Josh were both on the mend; Billy was now clear of his law troubles; and Clyde was certain he'd managed to confuse their trail back to Red Horse enough so that it would take Billings a while to locate them.

So the three friends enjoyed steaks with baked potatoes and fried onions and corn. As always, Miss Amy's food was wonderful. There were buttermilk biscuits alongside a crock of fresh-churned butter that might've been the best Clyde ever tasted.

"Deputy Israel," grinned Josh Fallon, "as your immediate superior, I hereby order you to marry Miss Amy and also to invite me and Billy to your house every week for Sunday dinner.

Forever."

"Miss Genevieve too!" added Billy. "Sounds like a plan to me," said Clyde, unaware that Miss Amy herself had come up to the table with the coffee pot, and was standing behind him.

"I heard that, Clyde," she teased him. It is hard for a black man to blush bright red but Clyde managed it. She patted his hand. "We can talk about it later, sugar." She put the coffee pot down and walked back to the kitchen chuckling to herself, leaving behind her a stunned silence. She put a little something extra in her walk because she knew Clyde was watching.

Clyde even surprised himself with what he said next. "You know, fellas, couple of weeks ago I was the town drunk. Today I got a good job and some good friends. Who knows what the future might bring? I b'lieve I'll miss my wife and my little boy until my dyin' day...but maybe I still got some life worth livin...'"

He shook his head decisively. "Can't be thinkin' 'bout that now," he declared. "Not until we deal with this Billings character."

All three men refused dessert, but Clyde asked Miss Amy if she would box up a pastry or two for Miss Genevieve, as the three men intended to stop by the doctor's and say hello if she was awake. Miss Amy gave Clyde a cardboard box with a ribbon tied in a bow and refused any payment. She gave Clyde a saucy wink. "You tell that young lady to hurry up and get well," she told him. "I'm going to need her to be my maid of honor now that you've proposed and all."

Clyde gulped. He knew when he was beaten. "I'll tell her," he promised.

As Clyde and Josh were leaving the restaurant, Billy separated from them. "I'll catch up with you at the doc's", he promised.

Genevieve was awake when Clyde and Josh entered the doctor's place, although she was a little groggy from the laudanum he'd given her. She told her friends about her ordeal. "The doctor took a metal rod, looked like the ramrod to an old flintlock rifle," she said. "He wrapped a piece of cloth around it and soaked it in alcohol. Then he ran it through my wound, front and back, and I pretty much passed out from the pain. When I came to, he was sewing the wounds closed with catgut. He said I'd be fine."

Somebody tapped at the door, and then Billy entered, carrying a Gladstone bag. "Howdy, Miss Genevieve," he smiled at the young lady. "Hi, Billy," she smiled back curiously. "What's in the bag?"

"Well, ma'am," he told her very seriously, "when the word got out that I was comin' to visit you, a friend of yours insisted on comin' along." He reached in the bag and pulled out a calico kitten. "L'il Bit says hello."

L'il Bit squirmed out of Billy's hands. She landed on Genevieve's belly and immediately began kneading biscuits, purring contentedly. Genevieve was delighted. "Thank you, Billy," she told him. "I love you and Clyde and Josh to pieces, but having my little sister here with me means the world."

The kitten had both eyes closed and was purring like a steam engine as Genevieve scratched her chin. Genevieve smiled wistfully, a little goofy from the laudanum. "I lost my family when I was ten," she mused. "Clyde and Billy lost their families to cholera, and Josh's parents were killed by Indians. God only knows how L'il Bit wound up alone so young. Maybe we were all destined to be some kind of Not Related by Blood family? Like a Related by Tragedy family?."

she fell asleep.

The three men and kitten snuck out quietly. "Let her get some rest," they reasoned.

"I like what Miss Genevieve said about us," Billy said thoughtfully. "Like we're a family even though not by blood. Haven't had that in a long long time, family, I mean."

Clyde thought abought it. "Two white law officers, a white ex-outlaw tryin' to go straight, a black ex-drunk tryin' to go sober, and a cat.

This's one colorful family we got goin' here!"

CHAPTER SEVENTEEN

WHILE CLYDE, JOSH and Billy were enjoying their dinner together at the Shoo-Fly Restaurant, Injun was riding out onto the desert from his hideout to intercept Billings and eight of his men. Injun led them back to his camp, which wasn't more than a crack in the rock where a little water trickled out, forming a small pool. He had a mostly-hidden hatful of fire built and there was some sparse graze for the horses. The men made coffee and ate biscuits and sliced beef they had brought along.

"Four of us took off west when the War ended," Billings mused as he sat by the fire, a flat pint of whiskey in his hand. "We lost one right away in Texas, another two years ago when that bitch gave me this scar...Johnson ran off to New York City and I'm the only one left...I gotta kill her before she kills me!"

"Don't worry, boss," Injun reassured him. "We'll get her. I got a plan..."

The boys split up after visiting Genevieve at the doctor's place. The deputy had his cot at the jail; Billy, Clyde and L'il Bit were staying at the stage station's livery stable, courtesy of Mister Newton. He had removed some tack and whatnot from a mostly-empty storage room and told them it was theirs for as long as they needed it. A black man, a jailbird and a stray kitten, yet Newton didn't hesitate to step up and help them. A damn good man.

First thing in the morning, Clyde was wide awake. Possibly the tiny calico kitten purring it's hot breath directly into Clyde's right ear woke him up. Or maybe it was the bright Arizona sunrise beaming through the window. Didn't matter. Clyde was wide awake, and unlike a few weeks ago, felt rested and alert instead of hungover and miserable. He played with L'il Bit for a few minutes, then got out of bed. He flexed his leg. The thigh wound was healing good. Maybe a little weak but definitely getting better. Clyde got dressed. He strapped on the belt with his revolver and knife but skipped his hat since he was only going down to the jailhouse for coffee. He glanced back as he quietly left the storeroom. Billy was sprawled across his cot sound asleep and L'il Bit was sprawled across Clyde's cot, fading fast.

Clyde grinned and shut the door behind him. At the doctor's office, something woke Genevieve. She lay in bed for a while listening. She didn't hear anything but somehow felt nervous anyway. She glanced at the head of the bed where her Smith and Wesson hung from the bedpost in it's gunbelt. Clyde, ever thoughtful, had cleaned and loaded it for her and left it near to her hand. She felt vastly comforted knowing it was there.

Clyde made a quick stop at the Shoo-Fly and picked up a bag of Miss Amy's bear sign. Then he ambled down the boardwalk to the jailhouse. As he was unlocking the door,

Injun and another man came quickly around the corner of the building. Injun already had his revolver reversed in his hand and he clouted Clyde across the head with the gun butt before Clyde had any idea what was happening. Injun's partner finished unlocking the door. He threw it open, gun drawn, in time to see Josh Fallon bolt upright in the cot in the unlocked jail cell he slep in. "Don't move!" barked Injun's partner, a young man with bad smallpox scars. He made sure Josh had no weapons in the cell, then locked him in. Meanwhile Injun was dragging Clyde into the jail. He thought Clyde was unconscious until Clyde suddenly threw off his hands and pushed him. The unexpected push to the chest sent Injun back out the doorway and off the steps. He fell on his back in the dusty street.

Inside the jail, the youth with the smallpox scars had turned his gun on Clyde, but in doing so, he got a little too close to the jail cell. Deputy Josh Fallon snaked out one arm and got him around the neck. He yanked him back against the cell bars and choked him unconscious. The young man fired one shot from his revolver before passing out, but it went harmlessly into the wood-planked floor.

Another of Billings' men came charging into the jailhouse with Injun right behind him. Clyde buried his fighting knife in the chest of the first man but Injun shot him in the head and he collapsed.

Injun staggered out of the jailhouse. He took three men and went up the street while Billings took the last three and went down. Injun hadn't gone more than fifty yards when there was the BOOM of a Sharps rifle. The head of the man standing next to him exploded. While Injun and his remaining two men were still standing frozen in shock, a second BOOM took out another man. This time, they could see from the puff of smoke that the shooter was at the livery. Injun dived into an alley but his last remaing man ducked behind a galvanized metal horse trough. Big mistake. A Sharps .50 could shoot through six inches of solid pine. The livery stable shooter fired twice right through the trough and Injun was out of men. Time to skedaddle.

Billings and his three men were way up the street by now. They could hear the gunshots behind them and imagined things weren't going well for Injun and his men. "Where IS that bitch?" Billings fumed aloud.

Suddenly the door to the doctor's office opened and Genevieve walked out into the street. She was wearing her clothes from the day before, with dried blood all over her shirt. She looked pale and weak but she had her pistol in her hand. "I'm right here," she said quietly, and as the four men turned, she began firing. Two of Billings' men had rifles so she shot them first. She saw the third man fall and was puzzled until she realized the Sharps had gotten him from up the street.

That left only Billings and Genevieve. They both shot at the same time. Billings missed completely, but Genevieve's bullet took him right between the eyes and he was dead before he hit the ground. Spent, she started back into the doctor's office to lay down.

Behind her, Injun scuttled out of an alley like a big spider, pistol in hand. He stopped in the street and planted his legs wide apart for balance. He aimed dead center between Genevieve's shoulder blades and cocked his pistol.

Genevieve heard the pistol cocking behind her. She knew she could never turn, draw, aim and fire in time to save her life but she had no choice. Even as she spun, she heard a thunk.

Injun was on his knees, then he fell forward onto his face. The hilt of Clyde's fighting knife stuck out of his back. Genevieve looked up.

Clyde was on one knee in the jailhouse doorway. The whole side of his head was bloody, but he was smiling.

"What you get for messin' with my family," he rasped.

Then he passed out.

But that was okay, because he woke up back in his cot in the jailhouse with a tiny calico kitten purring in his ear and his friends all waiting patiently to make sure he'd be all right.

Hello! I hope you enjoyed reading Anomaly Jane as much as I enjoyed writing it. If you did, please be kind enough to leave a quick review HERE. Reviews mean everything to authors!

You might also enjoy my books The Sackett Pistol and Jim Lane: Vengeance Trail, which you can find by clicking HERE.

If you'd like to chat, I love reader feedback! My email is lincolnkeenewriter@gmail.com.

See you somewhere down the trail!

Lincoln Keene 2022